Adeline Dutton Train Whitney

Mother Goose

For Grown Folks

Adeline Dutton Train Whitney

Mother Goose
For Grown Folks

ISBN/EAN: 9783744769280

Printed in Europe, USA, Canada, Australia, Japan

Cover: Foto ©Andreas Hilbeck / pixelio.de

More available books at **www.hansebooks.com**

MOTHER GOOSE FOR GROWN FOLKS

A CHRISTMAS READING.

MOTHER GOOSE

FOR GROWN FOLKS

BY

Mrs. A. D. T. WHITNEY

NEW, REVISED, AND ENLARGED EDITION, ILLUS-
TRATED BY AUGUSTUS HOPPIN

BOSTON AND NEW YORK
HOUGHTON, MIFFLIN AND COMPANY
The Riverside Press, Cambridge
1900

The Riverside Press, Cambridge, Mass., U. S. A.
Electrotyped and Printed by H. O. Houghton & Company

CONTENTS.

—◆—

iv CONTENTS.

CONTENTS.

LIST OF ILLUSTRATIONS.

———◆———

INTRODUCTORY.

Somewhere in that uncertain "long ago,"
　　Whose dim and vague chronology is all
That elfin tales or nursery fables know,
Rose a rare spirit, — keen, and quick, and
　　　　quaint, —
Whom by the title, whether fact or feint,
　　Mythic or real, Mother Goose we call.

Of Momus and Minerva sprang the birth
That gave the laughing oracle to earth:

1

A brimming bowl she bears, that, frothing
    high
  With sparkling nonsense, seemeth non-
    sense all;
Till, the bright, floating syllabub blown by,
Lo, in its ruby splendor doth upshine
The crimson radiance of Olympian wine
  By Pallas poured, in Jove's own banquet-
    hall.

The world was but a baby when she came;
So to her songs it listened, and her name
Grew to a word of power, her voice a spell
With charm to soothe its infant wearying
    well.
But, in a later and maturer age,
Developed to a dignity more sage,
Having its Shakspeares and its Words-
    worths now.

Its Southeys and its Tennysons, to wear
A halo on the high and lordly brow,
Or poet-laurels in the waving hair;
Its Lowells, Whittiers, Longfellows, to sing
Ballads of beauty, like the notes of spring,
The wise and prudent ones to nursery use
Leave the dear lyrics of old Mother Goose.

Wisdom of babes, — the nursery Shak-
    speare still, —.
Cackles she ever with the same good-will:
Uttering deep counsels in a foolish guise,
That come as warnings, even to the wise;
As when, of old, the martial city slept,
Unconscious of the wily foe that crept
Under the midnight, till the alarm was heard
Out from the mouth of Rome's plebeian
    bird.

Full many a rare and subtile thing hath
    she,
Undreamed of in the world's philosophy:
Toss-balls for children hath she humbly
    rolled,
That shining jewels secretly enfold;
Sibylline leaves she casteth on the air,
Twisted in fool's-caps, blown unheeded by,
That, in their lines grotesque, albeit, bear
Words of grave truth, and signal prophecy;
And lurking satire, whose sharp lashes hit
A world of follies with their homely wit;
With here and there a roughly uttered hint,
That makes you wonder at the beauty
    in't;
As if, along the wayside's dusty edge,
A hot-house flower had blossomed in a
    hedge.

So, like brave Layard in old Nineveh,

Among the memories of ancient song,

As curious relics, I would fain bestir;

And gather, if it might be, into strong

    And shapely show, some wealth of its
        lost lore;

Fragments of Truth's own architecture,
        strewed

In forms disjointed, whimsical, and rude,

That yet, to simpler vision, grandly stood

    Complete, beneath the golden light of
        yore!

BRAHMIC.

If a great poet think he sings,
  Or if the poem think it's sung,
They do but sport the scattered plumes
  That Mother Goose aside hath flung.

Far or forgot to me is near:
  Shakspeare and Punch are all the same;
The vanished thoughts do reappear,
  And shape themselves to fun or fame.

They use my *quills*, and leave me out,
  Oblivious that I wear the *wings*;

Or that a Goose has been about,
  When every little gosling sings.

Strong men may strive for grander thought,
  But, six times out of every seven,
My old philosophy hath taught
  All they can master this side heaven.

LITTLE BOY BLUE.

"Little boy blue! come blow your horn!
  The sheep in the meadow, the cows in the corn!
  Where's little boy blue, that looks after the sheep?
  He's under the hay-mow, fast asleep!"

Of morals in novels, we've had not a few;
With now and then novel moralities too;
And we've weekly exhortings from pulpit
      to pew;
But it strikes me, — and so it may chance
      to strike you, —
Scarce any are better than "Little Boy
      Blue."

For the veteran dame knows her business
    right well,
And her quaint admonitions unerringly
    tell:
She strings a few odd, careless words in a
    jingle,
And the sharp, latent truth fairly makes
    your ears tingle.

"Azure-robed Youth!" she cries, "up to
    thy post!
And watch, lest thy wealth be all scattered
    and lost:
Silly thoughts are astray, beyond call of
    the horn,
And passion breaks loose, and gets into the
    corn!

Is this the way Conscience looks after her
    sheep ?
In the world's soothing shadow, gone sound-
    ly asleep ? "

Is n't *that*, now, a sermon ?   No lengthened
    vexation
Of heads, and divisions, and argumenta-
    tion,
But a straightforward leap to the sure ap-
    plication ;
And, though many a longer harangue is
    forgot,
Of which careful reporters take notes on
    the spot,
I think, — as the " Deacon " declared of his
    " shay,"

Put together for lasting for ever and aye, —
A like immortality holding in view,
The old lady's discourse will undoubtedly
    "dew"!

HICCORY, DICCORY, DOCK.

―――――

" Hiccory, diccory, dock !
The mouse ran up the clock.
The clock struck one, and down she run :
Hiccory, diccory, dock ! "

She had her simple nest in a safe and cun-
ning place,
Away down in the quiet of the deep, old-
fashioned case.
A little crevice nibbled out led forth into
the world,
And overhead, on busy wheels, the hours
and minutes whirled.

High up in mystic glooms of space was
awful scenery
Of wires, and weights, and springs, and all
great Time's machinery;

13

But she had nought to do with these; a
    blessed little mouse,
Whose only care beneath the sun was just
    to keep her house.

For this was all she knew, or could; with-
    out her, just the same
The earth's great centre drew the weight;
    the pendulum went and came;
And days were born, and grew, and died;
    and stroke by stroke were told
The hours by which the world and men
    are ever growing old.

It suddenly occurred to her, — it struck her
    all at once, —
That living among things of power, her-
    self had been a dunce.

"Somebody winds the clock!" she cried
  "Somebody comes and brings
An iron finger that feels through and fum-
  bles at the springs;

"And then it happens; then the buzz is
  stirred afar and near,
And the hour sounds, and everywhere the
  great world stops to hear.
I don't think, after all, it seems so hard a
  thing to do.
I know the way — I might run up and
  make folks listen too."

She sprang upon the leaden weight; but
  not the merest whit
Did all her added gravity avail to hurry it.
She clambered up the steady cord; it wav-
  ered not a hair.
She got among the earnest wheels; they
  knew not she was there.

She sat beside the silent bell; the patient
      hammer lay
Waiting an unseen bidding for the word
      that it should say.
Only a solemn whisper thrilled the cham-
      bers of the clock,
And the mouse listened: " Hiccory! hic—
      diccory! dic — dock!"

Something was coming. She had hit the
      ripeness of the time;
No tiny second was outreached by that ex-
      ultant climb;
In no wise did the planet turn the faster to
      the sun;
She only met the instant, but the great
      clock sounded —" One!"

What then?   Did she stand gloriously
    among those central things,
Her eye upon the vibrant bell, her heel
    upon the springs?
Was her soul grand in unison with that
    resounding chime,
And her pulse-beat identical with the high
    pulse of Time?

Ah, she was little!   When the air first
    shattered with that shock,
Down ran the mouse into her hole.   "Hic,
    diccory! dic — dock!"
Too plain to be translated is the truth the
    tale would show,
Small souls, in solemn upshot, had better
    wait below.

BO-PEEP.

    " Little Bo-Peep
      Has lost her sheep,
  And does n't know where to find 'em
      Let 'em alone,
      And they 'll come home,
  And bring their tails behind 'em."

Hope beckoned Youth, and bade him keep,
On Life's broad plain, his shining sheep,
And while along the sward they came,
He called them over, each by name;
This one was Friendship,—that was Health;
Another Love,—another Wealth;

One, fat, full-fleeced, was Social Station;
Another, stainless, Reputation;
In truth, a goodly flock of sheep, —
A goodly flock, but hard to keep.

Youth laid him down beside a fountain;
Hope spread his wings to scale a mountain;
And, somehow, Youth fell fast asleep,
And left his crook to tend the sheep:
No wonder, as the legend says,
They took to very crooked ways.

He woke — to hear a distant bleating, —
The faithless quadrupeds were fleeting!

Wealth vanished first, with stealthy tread,
Then Friendship followed — to be fed, —
And foolish Love was after led;

Fair Fame, — alas ! some thievish scamp
Had marked him with his own black stamp !
And he, with Honor at his heels,
Was out of sight across the fields.

Health just hangs doubtful, — distant Hope
Looks backward from the mountain slope, —
And Youth himself — no longer Youth —
Stands face to face with bitter Truth.

Yet let them go !   'T were all in vain
    To linger here in faith to find 'em ;
Forward ! — nor pause to think of pain, —
Till somewhere, on a nobler plain,
A surer Hope shall lead the train
Of joys withheld to come again
    With golden fleeces trailed behind 'em !

SOLOMON GRUNDY.

" Solomon Grundy
　Born on Monday,
　　Christened on Tuesday,
　　Married on Wednesday,
　　Sick on Thursday,
　　Worse on Friday,
　　Dead on Saturday,
　　Buried on Sunday :
　　This was the end
　　Of Solomon Grundy."

So sings the unpretentious Muse
That guides the quill of Mother Goose,
And in one week of mortal strife
Presents the epitome of Life :

But down sits Billy Shakspeare next,
And, coolly taking up the text,
His thought pursues the trail of mine,
And, lo! the "Seven Ages" shine!
O world! O critics! *can't* you see
How Shakspeare plagiarizes me?

And other bards will after come,
    To echo in a later age,
"He lived, — he died: behold the sum,
    The abstract of the historian's page"; —
Yet once for all the thing was done,
    Complete in Grundy's pilgrimage.

For not a child upon the knee
But hath the moral learned of me;
And measured, in a seven days' span,
The whole experience of man.

BOWLS.

"Three wise men of Gotham
Went to sea in a bowl:
If the bowl had been stronger,
My song had been longer."

MYSTERIOUSLY suggestive! A vague hint,
    Yet a rare touch of most effective art,
That of the bowl, and all the voyagers in 't,
    Tells nothing, save the fact that they did
        start.
There ending suddenly, with subtle craft,
The story stands, — as 't were a broken
        shaft, —

More eloquent in mute signification,
Than lengthened detail, or precise relation.
So perfect in its very non-achieving,
That, of a truth, I cannot help believing
A rash attempt at paraphrasing it
May prove a blunder, rather than a hit.

Still, I must wish the venerable soul
Had been explicit as regards the *bowl.*
Was it, perhaps, a railroad speculation?
Or a big ship to carry all creation,
That, by some kink of its machinery,
Failed, in the end, to carry even three?
Or other fond, erroneous calculation
Of splendid schemes that died disastrously?

It must have been of Gotham manufacture;
Though strangely weak, and liable to frac-
  ture.

Yet — pause a moment — strangely, did I
　　say?
Scarcely, since, after all, it was but clay; —
The stuff Hope takes to build her brittle
　　boat,
And therein sets the wisest men afloat.
Truly, a bark would need be somewhat
　　stronger,
To make the halting history much longer.

Doubtless, the good Dame did but gener-
　　alize, —
Took a broad glance at human enterprise,
And earthly expectation, and so drew,
In pithy lines, a parable most true, —
Kindly to warn us ere we sail away,
With life's great venture, in an ark of
　　clay,

Where shivered fragments all around be-
        token,
How even the "golden bowl" at last lies
        broken!

CRADLED IN GREEN.

" Rockaby, baby,
 Your cradle is green;
Father 's a nobleman,
 Mother 's a queen;
And Betty 's a lady,
 And wears a gold ring,
And Johnny 's a drummer,
 And drums for the king!"

O GOLDEN gift of childhood!
That, with its kingly touch,
Transforms to more than royalty
The thing it loveth much!

O second sight, bestowed alone
    Upon the baby seer,
That the glory held in Heaven's reserve
    Discerneth even here!

Though he be the humblest craftsman,
    No silk nor ermine piled
Could make the father seem a whit
    More noble to the child;
And the mother,—ah, what queenlier crown
    Could rest upon her brow,
Than the fair and gentle dignity
    It weareth to him now?

E'en the gilded ring that Michael
    For a penny fairing bought,
Is the seal of Betty's ladyhood
    To his untutored thought;

And the darling drum about his neck, —
  His very newest toy, —
A bandsman unto Majesty
  Hath straightway made the boy!

O golden gift of childhood!
  If the talisman might last,
How the dull Present still should gleam
  With the glory of the Past!
But the things of earth about us
  Fade and dwindle as we go,
And the long perspective of our life
  Is truth, and not a show!

"SIMILIA SIMILIBUS."

"There was a man in our town,
And he was wondrous wise:
He jumped into a bramble-bush,
And scratched out both his eyes.
But when he saw his eyes were out,
With all his might and main
He jumped into another bush,
And scratched them in again!"

OLD Dr. Hahnemann read the tale,
(And he was wondrous wise,)
Of the man who, in the bramble-bush,
Had scratched out both his eyes.

And the fancy tickled mightily
    His misty German brain,
That, by jumping in another bush,
    He got them back again.

So he called it " homo-hop-athy " ·
    And soon it came about,
That a curious crowd among the thorns
    Was hopping in and out.
Yet, disguise it by the longest name
    They may, it is no use ;
For the world knows the discovery
    Was made by Mother Goose !

And not alone in medicine
    Doth the theory hold good :
In Life and in Philosophy,
    The maxim still hath stood :

A morsel more of anything,
　　When one has got enough,
And Nature's energy disowns
　　The whole unkindly stuff.

A second negative affirms;
　　And two magnetic poles
Of charge identical, repel,—
　　As sameness sunders souls.
Touched with a first, fresh suffering,
　　All solace is despised;
But gathered sorrows grow serene,
　　And grief is neutralized.

And he who, in the world's *mêlée,*
　　Hath chanced the worse to catch,
May mend the matter, if he come
　　Back, boldly, to the scratch;

Minding the lesson he received
   In boyhood, from his mother,
Whose cheery word, for many a bump,
   Was, Up and take another!

HOBBY-HORSES.

"I had a little pony,
   His name was Dapple Gray:
I lent him to a lady
   To ride a mile away.
She whipped him,
   She lashed him,
She rode him through the mire;
I wouldn't lend my pony now,
For all the lady's hire."

Our hobbies, of whatever sort
   They be, mine honest friend,
Of fancy, enterprise, or thought,
   'T is hardly wise to lend.

Some fair imagination, shrined
   In form poetic, maybe,
You fondly trusted to the World,—
   That most capricious Lady.

Or a high, romantic theory,
   Magnificently planned,
In flush of eager confidence
   You bade her take in hand.

But she whipped it, and she lashed it,
   And bespattered it with mire,
Till your very soul felt stained within,
   And scourged with stripes of fire.

Yet take this thought, and hold it fast,
   Ye Martyrs of To-day!
That same great World, with all its scorn,
   You're lifted on its way!

MISSIONS.

"Hogs in the garden,—
Catch 'em, Towser!
Cows in the cornfield,—
Run, boys, run!
Fire on the mountains,—
Run, boys, run boys!
Cats in the cream-pot,—
Run, girls, run!"

I DON'T stand up for Woman's Right;
Not I,—no, no!
The real lionesses fight,—
I let it go.

Yet, somehow, as I catch the call
    Of the world's voice,
That speaks a summons unto all
    Its girls and boys;

In such strange contrast still it rings
    As church-bells' bome
To the pert sound of tinkling things
    One hears at home;
And wakes an impulse, not germane
    Perhaps, to woman,
Yet with a thrill that makes it plain
    'T is truly human; —

A sudden tingle at the springs
    Of noble feeling,
The spirit-power for valiant things
    Clearly revealing.

But Eden's curse doth daily deal
　　Its certain dole, —
And the old grasp upon the heel
　　Holds back the soul!

So, when some rousing deed 's to do,
　　To save a nation,
Or, on the mountains, to subdue
　　A conflagration,
Woman! the work is not for you;
　　Mind your vocation!
Out from the cream-pot comes a mew
　　Of tribulation!

Meekly the world's great exploits leave
　　Unto your betters;
So bear the punishment of Eve,
　　Spirit in fetters!

Only, the hidden fires will glow,
  And, now and then,
A beacon blazeth out below
  That startles men!

Some Joan, through battle-field to stake,
  Danger embracing;
Some Florence, for sweet mercy's sake
  Pestilence facing;
Whose holy valor vindicates
  The royal birth
That, for its crowning, only waits
  The end of earth;
And, haply, when we all stand freed,
  In strength immortal,
Such virgin-lamps the host shall lead
  Through heaven's portal!

GOING BACK TO OUR MUTTONS.

" There was an old man of Tobago,
   Who lived on rice, gruel, and sago,
      Till, much to his bliss,
      His physician said this:
   To a leg, sir, of mutton, you may go.
   He set a monkey to baste the mutton,
   And ten pounds of butter he put on."

" CHAIN up a child, and away he will go ";
I have heard of the proverb interpreted so;
The spendthrift is son to the miser, — and
    still,
When the Devil would work his most piti-
    less will,

He sends forth the seven, for such embas-
    sies kept,
To the house that is empty and garnished
    and swept:
For poor human nature a pendulum seems,
That must constantly vibrate between two
    extremes.

The closer the arrow is drawn to the
    bow,
Once slipped from the string, all the further
    't will go:
Let a panic arise in the world of finance,
And the mad flight of Fashion be checked
    by the chance,
It certainly seems a most wonderful thing,
When the ropes are let go again, how it
    will swing!

And even the decent observance of Lent,

Stirs sometimes a doubt how the time has
  been spent,

When Easter brings out the new bonnets
  and gowns,

And a flood of gay colors o'erflows in the
  towns.

So in all things the feast doth still follow
  the fast,

And the force of the contrast gives zest to
  the last;

And until he is tried, no frail mortal can
  tell,

The inch being offered, he won't take the
  ell.

We are righteously shocked at the follies
  of fashion;

Nay, standing outside, may get quite in a
        passion
    At the prodigal flourishes other folks put
        on:
But many good people this side of Tobago,
If respited once from their diet of sago,
    Would outdo the monkey in basting the
        mutton!

GOING TO DOVER.

―――――

" Leg over leg
    As the dog went to Dover ;
  When he came to a stile,
    Jump he went over."

PERHAPS you would n't see it here,
But, to my fancy, 't is quite clear
That Mother Goose just meant to show
How the dog Patience on doth go:
With steadfast nozzle, pointing low,—-
Leg over leg, however slow,—
And labored breath, but naught complaining,
Still, at each footstep, somewhat gaining,—

Quietly plodding, mile on mile,
   And gathering for a nervous bound
At every interposing stile,—
   So traversing the tedious ground,
Till all, at length, he measures over,
And walks, a victor, into Dover.

And, verily, no other way
Doth human progress win the day;
Step after step,—and o'er and o'er,—
Each seeming like the one before
So that 't is only once a while,—
When sudden Genius springs the stile
That marks a section of the plain,
Beyond whose bound fresh fields again
Their widening stretch untrodden sweep,—
The world looks round to see the leap.

Pale Science, in her laboratory,
    Works on with crucible and wire
Unnoticed, till an instant glory
    Crowns some high issue, as with fire,
And men, with wondering eyes awide,
Gauge great Invention's giant stride.

No age, no race, no single soul,
By lofty tumbling gains the goal.
The steady pace it keeps between, —
The little points it makes unseen, —
By these, achieved in gathering might,
It moveth on, and out of sight,
And wins, through all that's overpast,
The city of its hopes at last.

RAGS AND ROBES.

———

" Hark, hark!
  The dogs do bark;
Beggars are coming to town:
  Some in rags,
  Some in tags,
And some in velvet gowns!"

COMING, coming always!
  Crowding into earth;
Seizing on this human life,
  Beggars from the birth.

Some in patent penury;
   Some, alas! in shame;
And some in fading velvet
   Of hereditary fame;

But all in deep, appeaseless want,
   As mendicants to live;
And go beseeching through the world,
   For what the world may give.

Beggars, beggars, all of us!
   Expectants from our youth:
With hands outstretched, and asking alms
   Of Hope and Love and Truth.

Nor, verily, doth he escape
   Who, wrapt in cold contempt,
Denies alike to give or take,
   And dreams himself exempt;

Who never, in appeal to man,
  Nor in a prayer to Heaven,
Will own that aught he doth desire,
  Or ask that aught be given.

Whose human heart a stoic pride
  Folds as a velvet pall;
Yet hides a meagreness within,
  Worse beggary than all!

———————

Coming, coming always!
  And the bluff Apostle waits
As the throng pours upward from the earth
  To Heaven's eternal gates.

In shreds of torn affection,
  In passion-rended rags;

4

While scarcely at the portal
    The great procession flags;

For the pillared doors of glory
    On their hinges hang awide;
Where each asking soul may enter,
    And at last be satisfied!

But a cold, calm shade arriveth,
    In self-complacent trim, —
And Peter riseth up to see
    Especially to him.

"Good morrow, saint! I'm going in
    To take a stroll, you know;
Not that *I want* for anything, —
    But just to see the show!"

"Hold!" thunders out the warden,
    "Be pleased to pause a bit!

For seats celestial, let me say,
 You 're not apparelled fit:
Yonder 's the brazen door that leads
 Spectators to the pit!

Whatever may be thought on earth,
 We 've other rules in heaven;
And only poverty confessed
 Finds free admittance given!"

BLACKBIRDS.

"Sing a song o' sixpence, a pocket full of rye;
  Four and twenty blackbirds baked in a pie:
  When the pie was opened, they all began to sing,
  And was n't this a dainty dish to set before the king?
  The king was in his counting-house, counting out his
      money;
  The queen was in the parlor, eating bread and honey;
  The maid was in the garden, hanging out the clothes,
  And along came a blackbird, and nipt off her nose!"

It does n't take a conjurer to see
The sort of curious pasty this might be;
A flock of flying rumors, caught alive,
And housed, like swarming bees within a
    hive, —

Instead of what were far more wisely
done,
Having their worthless necks wrung, every
one;—
And so a dish of dainty gossip making,
Smooth covered with a show of secrecy,
That one but takes the pleasant pains of
breaking,
And out the wide-mouthed knaves pop,
eagerly.

Blackbirds, indeed! Each chattering *on-
dit*
Comes forth, full feathered, black as black
can be;
With quivering throats, all tremulous to
sing,
And please, forsooth, some little social
king;

Whose reign may last as long as he is able
To call his court around a dinner-table.

But, mark the sequel! When the laugh is
        over,
Think not to get the varlets under cover:
The crust once broken, you may seek in vain
To catch the birds, or coax them in again;
Mrs. Pandora's famous box, I wis,
Was nothing worse than such a pie as this:
And so, some pleasant morning, — when,
        down town,
    The king is busy with his bags of money,
Leaving at home the queenly Mrs. Brown
    Safe at her breakfast of fair bread and
        honey, —
Some quiet, harmless soul, who never
        knows
    Of any matters, save the plain pursuing

Her daily round, — the hanging out of
    clothes
Or other lawful work she may be doing, —
Finds, by the sudden nipping of her nose,
    What sort of mischief is about her brew-
        ing !

Not that, indeed, there's anything to hinder
The thieves from flying though the parlor
    window;
For never yet could sentinel or warden
Keep scandals wholly to the kitchen gar-
    den.

When, therefore, as not seldom it may be,
Even in the soberest community,
Strange revelations somehow get about, —
Like a mysterious cholera breaking out

Sudden, as Egypt's blains 'neath Aaron's **rod**,

Contagious by a whisper or a nod, —

When daily papers teem with many a hint

That daubs them darker even than their
      print;

When it would seem, in short, the very
      D——

Had let his little imps out on a spree;

Conclude, beyond a reasonable doubt,

Although, perhaps, you fail to trace it out,

Such plagues spring not unbidden from the
      ground,

And, if the thing were sifted, 't would be
      found

Somebody's sown a pocket full of rye,

Or been regaling on a blackbird pie!

BANBURY CROSS.

" Ride a fine horse
　　　To Banbury Cross,
　　To see a young woman
　　　Jump on a white horse.
　Rings on her fingers,
　　　And bells on her toes,
　And she shall have music
　　　Wherever she goes."

Prophetic Dame!　What hadst thou in thy
　　view?
A modern wedding in Fifth Avenue?

Where,—like the goddess of a heathen
shrine,
With offerings heaped in such a glittering
show
As must have emptied a Peruvian mine,
And would suggest, but that we better
know,
Marriage must be a bitter thing indeed,
And, like the Prophet of the Eastern tale,
Must wear a very ugly face, to need
Such careful shrouding in the silver
veil,—
Her bridal pomp, as a white palfrey, mount-
ing,
Caparisoned at cost beyond all counting,
With diamond-jewelled fingers, and the
toes
Ditto, for all that anybody knows,

The smiling damsel goeth to the Banns?
   (Why add the "bury," or suggest the
      " cross,"
As if such brilliant ringing of the hands
   Preluded aught of trial or of loss?)

Shall not Life's golden bells still tinkle
      sweet,
And merry music make about her feet?
Shall not the silver sheen around her spread,
A lasting light along her pathway shed?

No mocking satire, surely, hides a sting,
   Nor bitter irony a truth foreshows,
In the gay chant the cheery dame doth
      sing, —
   "She shall have music wheresoe'er she
      goes"?

She shall have music!   Shall she sit apart,
 And let the folly-chimes outvoice the
  tone
That comes up wailing to the listening
  heart,
 From the great world, where misery
  maketh moan?
Ah, Mother Goose! if such the tale it tells,
Sing us no more your rhyme of rings and
  bells!

But may not—'t were a rare device in-
  deed!—
The wondrous oracle in both ways read?
And call up, as a fair beatitude,
The gracious vision of true womanhood,
That with pure purpose, and a gentle might,
Upheld and borne, as by the steed of white,

Pledged with her golden ring, goes nobly
    forth
To trace her path of joy along the earth, —
And, as she moves, makes music, silver-shod
" With preparation of the peace " of God,
That holds the key-note of celestial cheer,
And hangs heaven's echoes round her foot-
    steps here?

ATTIC SALT.

" Two little blackbirds sat upon a hill,
  One named Jack, the other named Jill;
  Fly away, Jack! fly away, Jill!
  Come again, Jack! come again, Jill!"

I HALF suspect that, after all,
  There's just the smallest bit
Of inequality between
  The witling and the wit.
'Tis only mental nimbleness:
  No language ever brought
A living word to soul of man
  But had the latent thought.

You may meet, among the million,
   Good people every day, —
Unconscious martyrs to their fate, —
   Who seem, in half they say,
On the brink of something brilliant
   They were almost sure to clinch,
Yet, by some queer freak of fortune,
   Just escape it by an inch!

I often think the selfsame shade, —
   This difference of a hair, —
Divides between the men of nought
   And those who do and dare.
An instant cometh on the wing,
   Bearing a kingly crown :
This man is dazzled and lets it by —
   That seizes and brings it down.

Winged things may stoop to any door
  Alighting close and low ;
And up and down, 'twixt earth and sky,
  Do always come and go.
Swift, fluttering glimpses touch us all,
  Yet, prithee, what avails?
'Tis only Genius that can put
  The salt upon their tails!

THE BIG SHOE.

"There was an old woman
    Who lived in a shoe;
She had so many children
    She did n't know what to do:
To some she gave broth,
    And to some she gave bread,
And some she whipped soundly,
    And sent them to bed."

Do you find out the likeness?
A portly old Dame, —
The mother of millions, —
Britannia by name:

And — howe'er it may strike you
  In reading the song —
Not stinted in space
  For bestowing the throng;
Since the Sun can himself
  Hardly manage to go,
In a day and a night,
  From the heel to the toe.

On the arch of the instep
  She builds up her throne,
And, with seas rolling under,
  She sits there alone;
With her heel at the foot
  Of the Himmalehs planted,
And her toe in the icebergs,
  Unchilled and undaunted.

Yet though justly of all
  Her fine family proud,
'Tis no light undertaking
  To rule such a crowd;
Not to mention the trouble
  Of seeing them fed,
And dispensing with justice
  The broth and the bread.
Some will seize upon one,—
  Some are left with the other,—
And so the whole household
  Gets into a pother.
But the rigid old Dame
  Has a summary way
Of her own, when she finds
  There is mischief to pay.
She just takes up the rod,
  As she lays down the spoon,

And makes their rebellious backs
    Tingle right soon :
Then she bids them, while yet
    The sore smarting they feel,
To lie down, and go to sleep,
    Under her heel !

Only once was she posed, —
    When the little boy Sam,
Who had always before
    Been as meek as a lamb,
Refused to take tea,
    As his mother had bid,
And returned saucy answers
    Because he was chid.

Not content even then,
    He cut loose from the throne,

And set about making
  A shoe of his own;
Which succeeded so well,
  And was filled up so fast,
That the world, in amazement,
  Confessed, at the last, —
Looking on at the work
  With a gasp and a stare, —
That 't was hard to tell which
  Would be best of the pair.

Side by side they are standing
  Together to-day;
Side by side may they keep
  Their strong foothold for aye:
And beneath the broad sea,
  Whose blue depths intervene,
May the finishing string
  Lie unbroken between!

VICTUALS AND DRINK.

"There once was a woman,
   And what do you think?
She lived upon nothing
   But victuals and drink.
Victuals and drink
   Were the chief of her diet,
And yet this poor woman
   Scarce ever was quiet."

AND were you so foolish
As really to think
That all she could want
Was her victuals and drink?

And that while she was furnished
  With that sort of diet,
Her feeling and fancy
  Would starve, and be quiet?

Mother Goose knew far better;
  But thought it sufficient
To give a mere hint
  That the fare was deficient;
For I do not believe
  She could ever have meant
To imply there was reason
  For being content.

Yet the mass of mankind
  Is uncommonly slow
To acknowledge the fact
  It behooves them to know;

Or to learn that a woman
　　Is not like a mouse,
Needing nothing but cheese,
　　And the walls of a house.

But just take a man, —
　　Shut him up for a day;
Get his hat and his cane, —
　　Put them snugly away;
Give him stockings to mend,
　　And three sumptuous meals; —
And then ask him, at night,
　　If you dare, how he feels!
Do you think he will quietly
　　Stick to the stocking,
While you read the news,
　　And " don't care about talking " ?

O, many a woman
  Goes starving, I ween,
Who lives in a palace,
  And fares like a queen;
Till the famishing heart,
  And the feverish brain,
Have spelled to life's end
  The long lesson of pain.

Yet, stay!   To my mind
  An uneasy suggestion
Comes up, that there may be
  Two sides to the question.
That, while here and there proving
  Inflicted privation,
The verdict must often be
  "Wilful starvation."

Since there *are* men and women
 Would force one to think
They *choose* to live only
 On victuals and drink.

O restless, and craving,
 Unsatisfied hearts,
Whence never the vulture
 Of hunger departs!
How long on the husks
 Of your life will ye feed,
Ignoring the soul,
 And her famishing need?

Bethink you, when lulled
 In your shallow content,
'T was to Lazarus only
 The angels were sent;

And 't is he to whose lips
  But earth's ashes are given,
For whom the full banquet
  Is gathered in heaven!

COBWEBS AND BROOMS.

"There was an old woman
Tossed up in a blanket,
Seventeen times as high as the moon;
What she did there
I cannot tell you,
But in her hand she carried a broom.
Old woman, old woman,
Old woman, said I,
O whither, O whither, O whither so high?
To sweep the cobwebs
Off the sky,
And I'll be back again, by and by."

MIND you, she wore no *wings*,
That she might truly *soar*; no time was lost

In growing such unnecessary things;
But blindly, in a blanket, she was *lost!*

Spasmodically, too!
'T was not enough that she should reach
the moon;
But seventeen times the distance she must
do,
Lest, peradventure, she get back too
soon.

That emblematic broom!
Besom of mad Reform, uplifted high,
That, to reach cobwebs, would precipitate
doom,
And sweep down thunderbolts from out
the sky!

Doubtless, no rubbish lay
About her door, — no work was there to
    do, —
That through the astonished aisles of Night
    and Day,
She took her valorous flight in quest of
    new !

Lo ! at her little broom
The great stars laugh, as on their wheels
    of fire
They go, dispersing the eternal gloom,
And shake Time's dust from off each
    blazing tire !

BLACK SPIDERS.

"Little Miss Muffet
Sat on a tuffet,
Eating curds and whey:
There came a black spider,
And sat down beside her,
And frightened Miss Muffet away."

To all mortal blisses,
From comfits to kisses,
There's sure to be something by way of
alloy;
Each new expectation
Brings fresh aggravation,
And a doubtful amalgam's the best of our
joy.

You may sit on your tuffet;

Yes, — cushion and stuff it;

And provide what you please, if you don't

    fancy whey;

But before you can eat it,

There 'll be — I repeat it —

Some sort of black spider to come in the

    way.

DAFFY-DOWN-DILLY.

———————

" Daffy-down-dilly
  Is new come to town,
  With a petticoat green,
    And a bright yellow gown,
  And her little white blossoms
    Are peeping around."

Now don't you call this
  A most exquisite thing ?
Don't it give you a thrill
  With the thought of the spring,
Such as once, in your childhood,
  You felt, when you found

The first yellow buttercups
   Spangling the ground?

When the lilac was fresh
   With its glory of leaves,
And the swallows came fluttering
   Under the eaves?
When the bluebird flashed by
   Like a magical thing,
And you looked for a fairy
   Astride of his wing?

When the clear, running water,
   Like tinkling of bells,
Bore along the bare roadside
   A song of the dells,—
And the mornings were fresh
   With unfailing delight,

While the sweet summer hush
　　Always came with the night?

O daffy-down-dilly,
　　With robings of gold!
As our hearts every year
　　To your coming unfold,
And sweet memories stir
　　Through the hardening mould,
We feel how earth's blossomings
　　Surely are given
To keep the soul fresh
　　For the spring-time of heaven!

BAA, BAA, BLACK SHEEP!

" Baa, baa, black sheep!
    Have you any wool?
Yes, sir, — no, sir, —
    Three bags full.
One for my master,
    One for my dame,
And one for the little boy
    That lives in the lane."

'T is the same question as of old;
    And still the doubter saith,
" Can any good be made to come
    From out of Nazareth?"

No sheep so black in all the flock, —
  No human heart so bare, —
But hath some warm and generous stock
  Of kindliness to share.

It may be treasured secretly
  For dear ones at the hearth;
Or be bestowed by stealth along
  The by-ways of the earth; —

And though no searching eye may see,
  Nor busy tongue may tell,
Perchance, where largest love is laid,
  The Master knoweth well!

THE TWISTER.

* A twister, in twisting, would twist him a twist,
And, twisting his twists, seven twists he doth twist:
If one twist, in twisting, untwist from the twist,
The twist, untwisting, untwists the twist."

A RAVELLED rainbow overhead
Lets down to life its varying thread:
Love's blue,—Joy's gold,—and, fair be-
       tween,
Hope's shifting light of emerald green;
With, either side, in deep relief,
A crimson Pain,—a violet Grief.

Wouldst thou, amid their gleaming hues,
Clutch after those, and these refuse?
Believe, — as thy beseeching eyes
Follow their lines, and sound the skies, —
There, where the fadeless glories shine,
An unseen angel twists the twine.

And be thou sure, what tint soe'er
The broken rays beneath may wear,
It needs them all, that, broad and white,
God's love may weave the perfect light!

FANTASY.

"I have a little sister,
   They call her peep, peep;
She wades through the water,
   Deep, deep, deep;
She climbs up the mountains,
   High, high, high;
My poor little sister,
   She has but one eye!"

Rough Common Sense doth here confess
   Her kinship to Imagination;
Betraying also, I should guess,
   Some little pride in the relation.

For even while vexed, and puzzled too,
By the vagaries of the latter, —
Fearful what next the child may do, —
She looks with loving wonder at her.

Plain Sense keeps ever to the road
That 's beaten down and daily trod;
While Fancy fords the rivers wide,
And scrambles up the mountain-side:
By which exploits she 's always getting
Either a tumble or a wetting.

While simple Sense looks straight before,
Fancy " peeps " further, and sees more;
And yet, if left to walk alone,
May chance, like most long-sighted people,
To trip her foot against a stone
While gazing at a distant steeple.

Nay, worse! with all her grace erratic,
And feats aerial and aquatic,
Her flights sublime, and moods ecstatic,
She of the vision wild and high
Hath but a solitary eye!
And, — not to quote the Scripture, which
Forebodes the falling in the ditch, —
Doubtless by following such a guide
Blindly, in all her wanderings wide,
The world, at best, would get o' one side.

What then?   To rid us of our doubt
   Is there no other thing to do
But we must turn poor Fancy out,
   And only downright Fact pursue?

Ah, see you not, bewildered man!
The heavenly beauty of the plan?

"T was so ordained, in counsels high,
To give to sweet Imagination
A single deep and glorious eye;
But then 't was meant, in compensation,
That Common Sense, with optics keen, —
As maid of honor to a queen, —
On her blind side should always stay,
And keep her in the middle way.

JINGLING AND JANGLING.

    " Little Jack Jingle
        Used to live single,
    But when he got tired
        Of that kind of life,
    He left off being single,
        And lived with his wife."

YOUR period's pointed, most excellent Moth-
        er!
Pray what did he do when he tired of the
        other?
For a man so deplorably prone to ennui
But a queer sort of husband is likely to be.

The fatigue might recur, — and, in case it
    should be so,
Why not take a wife on a limited lease, O ?
Grant the privilege, pray, to his idiosyn-
    crasy, —
Some natures won't bear to be too closely
    pinned, you see, —
And, at worst, the poor Benedict might
    advertise,
When weary, at length, of the light of his
    eyes, —
Or failing to find her, it may be, in salt, —
" Disposed of, indeed, for no manner of
    fault,"
(To borrow a figure of speech from the
    mart,)
" But because the late owner has taken a
    start ! "

I believe once before you have cautiously
    said

Something quite as concise on this delicate
    head,

When distantly hinting at "needles and
    pins,"

And that "when a man marries, his trouble
    begins";

But I don't recollect that you ever pretend

To prophesy anything as to the *end*.

Unless we may learn it of Peter, — the
    bumpkin,

Renowned for naught else but his eating
    of pumpkin;

Whose wife — I don't see how he happened
    to get her —

Had a taste, very likely, for things that
    were better:

Since, fearing to lose her, at last it befell

He bethought him of shutting her up in a
shell;

By which brilliant contrivance she *kept* very
well!

What he did with her next, the old rhyme
does n't say,

But she seems to be somehow got out of
the way,

For the ill-fated Peter was wedded once
more,

To find his bewilderment worse than before;

If the first for her spouse had but small
predilection,

Now 't was his turn, alas! to fall short in
affection.

And how do you think that he conquered
    the evil?

Why, simply by *lifting himself to her level;*

By leaving his pumpkins, and learning to
    spell,

He came, saith the story, to love her right
    well;

And the mythical memoir its moral con-
    trives

For the lasting instruction of husbands
    and wives.

THE OLD WOMAN OF SURREY.

"There was an old woman in Surrey,
Who was morn, noon, and night in a hurry;
Called her husband a fool,
Drove the children to school,
The worrying old woman of Surrey."

'T was an ancient earldom over the sea,
And it must be now as it used to be;
Yet the sketch is of one I have known
before, —
The very old woman that lives next door.

7

One   thing   is   unquestionable, — she 's
    " smart," —
As they say of an apple that 's rather tart ;
For her nearest friends, I think, would
    allow her
To be, at her best, but a " pleasant sour."

There 's a certain electrical atmosphere
That you feel beforehand, when she 's near :
And — unless you 've a wonderful deal of
    pluck —
A   shrinking   fear   that   you   might   be
    " struck."

She moves with such a bustle and rush, —
Such an elemental stir and crush,
As makes the branches bend and fall
In the breeze that blows up a thunder-squall.

And yet, it is only her endless " hurry ";
She 's not so bad if she would n't " worry,"
And, for all the worlds that she has to make,
If the six days' time she 'd only take.

You may talk about Surrey, or Devon, or
    Kent,
But I doubt if a special location was meant;
It may sound severe, — but it seems to me
That a " representative " woman was she ;

And that here and there you may chance
    to trace
Some specimens extant of the race :
For a slip of the stock, as I 've a notion,
Somehow "in the Mayflower" crossed the
    ocean.

PICKLE PEPPERS.

"Peter Piper picked a peck of pickle peppers;
   And a peck of pickle peppers Peter Piper picked;
If Peter Piper picked a peck of pickle peppers
   Where's the peck of pickle peppers Peter Piper
      picked?"

Poor Peter toiled his life away,
That afterward the world might say
"Where is the peck of peppers he
Did gather so industriously?"
The peppers are embalmed in metre, —
But who, alas! inquires for Peter?

In sun or storm, by night and day,
Scant time for sleep, and none for play,
Still the poor fool did nothing reck,
If only he might pick his peck :
And what result from all hath sprung,
But just to bite somebody's tongue?
Or, — Lady Fortune playing fickle, —
Get some one in a precious pickle?

HUMPTY DUMPTY.

"Humpty Dumpty sat on a wall:
Humpty Dumpty had a great fall:
Not all the king's horses nor all the king's men
Could set Humpty Dumpty up again."

Full many a project that never was hatched
Falls down, and gets shattered beyond be-
    ing patched;
And luckily, too! for if all came to chick-
    ens,
Then things without feathers might go to
    the dickens.

If each restless unit that moves among men
Might climb to a place with the privileged
    " ten,"
Pray tell us where all the commotion would
    stop!
Must the whole pan of milk, forsooth, rise
    to the top?

If always the statesman attained to his hopes,
And grasped the great helm, who would
    stand by the ropes?
Or if all dainty fingers their duties might
    choose,
Who would wash up the dishes, and polish
    the shoes?

Suppose every aspirant writing a book
Contrived to get published, by hook or by
    crook ;

Geologists then of a later creation

Would be startled, I fancy, to find a forma-
tion

Proving how the poor world did most wo-
fully sink

Beneath mountains of paper, and oceans of
ink !

Or even suppose all the women were married ;

By whom would superfluous babies be carried ?

Where would be the good aunts that should
knit all the stockings ?

Or nurses, to do up the singings and rock-
ings ?

Wise spinsters, to lay down their wonderful
rules,

And with theories rare to enlighten the
  fools, —
Or to look after orphans, and primary
  schools?

No! Failure's a part of the infinite plan;
Who finds that he can't, must give way to
  who can;
And as one and another drops out of the
  race,
Each stumbles at last to his suitable place.

So the great scheme works on, — though,
  like eggs from the wall,
Little single designs to such ruin may fall,
That not all the world's might, of its horses
  or men,
Could set their crushed hopes at the sum-
  mit again.

SUNDAY AND MONDAY.

"As Tommy Snooks and Bessy Brooks
   Were walking out one Sunday,
  Says Tommy Snooks to Bessy Brooks,
   To-morrow will be Monday."

No doubt you are smiling at such a remark,
And thinking poor Snooks but a pitiful
    spark;
But the words have a meaning, worth look-
    ing for, too,
As I'll presently try and demonstrate for
    you.

'T was a pity, indeed, in that moment of
leisure,
To dampen poor Bessy's hebdomadal pleas.
ure,
Suggesting that close on the beautiful Sunday
Must come all the common-place horrors
of Monday ;

That he to his toiling, and she to her
tub,
Must turn, and take up with another week's
rub ;
Yet a truth for us all, since the shade of
the real
Follows fast on the track of each sunny
ideal.

Now and then we may pause on Life's
    pleasant oases;
But between lie the desert's grim, desolate
    spaces;
And our feet, with all patience, must trav-
    erse them still,
Reaching forward to blessing, through
    bearing of ill.

Yet for Snooks and his Bessy,— for me
    and for you,—
Comes a Saturday night when the wage
    will be due;
And we'll say to each other, in ecstasy,
    one day,
" To-morrow — the endless to-morrow — is
    Sunday ! "

THE MAD HORSE.

"There was a mad man,
And he had a mad wife,
And the children were mad beside;
So on a mad horse
They all of them got,
And madly away did ride."

SAGACIOUS Goose!   Fresh wonders yet!
What spell had power to help you get
Those seven-leagued spectacles, that see
Down to the nineteenth century?

"The mad world, and his madder wife!"
That, in your earlier time of life, —
Though quite demented now, 't is plain, —
Were sober, grave, and almost sane!

109

And all the tribes, a motley brood
Sprung into being since the flood,
With their hereditary bent
To cerebral bewilderment!

If some old ghost, precise and slow,
Who died a hundred years ago, —
Always supposing he himself
Has lain, meanwhile, upon the shelf, —

Things as they are might only see,
Surely his inference would be
A simultaneous bursting out
Of lunacy the earth about.

"The world is mad; his wife is mad;
   The rising generation 's madder;"
And when a charter can be had,
   Up to the moon they 'll build a ladder!

They caught a horse awhile ago, —
They called him Steam, — but he was
  slow;
After the lightning then they ran,
Caught him, — and now they drive the
  span!   —1860.

   P. S. — 1870.

The great Pacific railroad 's done;
They 've poured two oceans into one;
Two shores with whispering cable tied,
And cut a path for ships to ride,
Where camel-tracks had used to be.
Through desert sands, from sea to sea.

Moon, quoth I?   Faith, they 've *made* a
  moon!
Leastwise, they 've *thought* one;[1] and so
  soon

[1] E. E. Hale's *Brick Moon:* likewise Jules Verne's *Projectile.*

Upon man's whim his stroke succeeds,
And turns his dreams into his deeds,
Look sharply! for with word and blow,
They 'll swing one up before you know!

,882.

Why put a double P. S. in?
'T would need a daily bulletin
To tell how fast the craze goes on,
With Keeley and with Edison;
With things to eat, and things to travel, —
Bicycles spinning o'er the gravel, —
Great guns to simplify the fights, —
Suns outshone with electric lights, —
The whisper in the closet stirred
In sooth across the housetops heard,
And when the airy tangle tires
Earth to be veined with throbbing wires.

Women to physic and to preach,
And help the national bird to screech;
One man on Wall-Street curb to stand,
With twenty railroads in his hand;
Schools for the mass, effecting this,
That all may know what most must miss!
Ah, who so sage that can pretend
To pre-sage of such tale the end?

I press the limit of my page;
So, haply, may this frantic age !

ROSES AND DIAMONDS.

"Little girl, little girl, where have you been?
    Gathering roses to give to the queen.
    Little girl, little girl, what gave she you?
    She gave me a diamond as big as my shoe."

IF the old could share with the young
    again, —
  If worn could borrow of new, —
If faces could wear their roses again,
  And hearts be sweetened with dew, —
If a child might bring the joy of a child,
  And give it to us to-day, —
What glory of gem, or what weight of gold
  Would we think too precious to pay?

114

JACK HORNER.

"Little Jack Horner
    Sat in a corner
   Eating a Christmas Pie:
    He put in his thumb,
    And pulled out a plum,
  And said, 'What a great boy am I!'"

Ah, the world hath many a Horner,
Who, seated in his corner,
Finds a Christmas Pie provided for his
    thumb:
And cries out with exultation,
When successful exploration
Doth discover the predestinated plum!

Little Jack outgrows his tier,
And becometh John, Esquire;
And he finds a monstrous pasty ready made,
Stuffed with stocks and bonds and bales,
Gold, currencies and sales,
And all the mixed ingredients of Trade.

And again it is his luck
To be just in time to pluck,
By a clever "operation," from the pie
An unexpected "plum";
So he glorifies his thumb,
And says, proudly, "What a mighty man
    am I!"

Or perchance, to Science turning,
And with weary labor learning
All the formulas and phrases that oppress
    her, —

For the fruit of others' baking
So a fresh diploma taking,
Comes he forth, a full accredited Profes-
sor!

Or he 's not too nice to mix
In the dish of politics;
And the dignity of office he puts **on;**
And he feels as big again
As a dozen nobler men,
While he writes himself the Honorable
John!

Ah, me, for the poor nation!
In her hour of desperation
Her worst foe is that unsparing Horner-
Thumb!
To which War, and Death, and Hate,
Right, Policy, and State,
Are but pies wherefrom his greed may
grasp a plum!

Oh, the work was fair and true,
But 't is riddled through and through,
And plundered of its glories everywhere;
And before men's cheated eyes
Doth the robber triumph rise
And magnify itself in all the air.

Why, if even a good man dies,
And is welcomed to the skies
In the glorious resurrection of the just,
They must ruffle it below
With some vain and wretched show,
To make each his little mud-pie of the dust!

Shall we hint at Lady-Horners,
Who in their exclusive corners
Think the world is only made of upper-
    crust?
Who in the queer mince-pie
That we call Society,
Do their dainty fingers delicately thrust;

Till, if it come to pass,
In the spiced and sugared mass,
One should compass, — do n't they call it
  so? — a *catch*,
By the gratulation given
It would seem the very heaven
Had outdone itself in making such a
  match!

Or the Woman-Horner, now,
Who is raising such a row
To prove that Jack's no bigger boy than
  Jill;
And that she wo n't sit by
With her little saucer pie,
While he from the Great Pasty picks his
  fill.

Jealous-wild to be a sharer
In the fruit she thinks the fairer,

Flings by all for the swift gaining of her
　　wish;
　Not discerning in her blindness,
　How a tender Loving-Kindness
Hid the best things in her own rejected
　　dish!

　O, the world keeps Christmas Day
　In a queer, perpetual way;
Shouting always, "What a great big boy
　　am I!"
　Yet how many of the crowd
　Thus vociferating loud,
And their honors or pretensions lifting
　　high,
　Have really, more than Jack,
　With their boldness or their knack,
Had a finger in the *making* of the Pie?

INTY, MINTY.

"Inty, minty,
   Cutey, corn!
Apple-seed,
   Apple-thorn!
Wire, brier,
   Limber lock;
Seven geese
   In a flock,
Sit and sing, by the spring;
O-u-t, out, and in again."

INKLINGS and meanings,
   Whispers and hints;
Sprinklings and gleanings,
   Shimmers and glints.

121

That 's how the light comes
　Down from the skies;
That 's how the beauty
　Is born to our eyes.

The seed is within,
　And the thorn is without:
Nature's sweet secret
　Is guarded about.
Yet briers are slender,
　Locks are but slight,
To touch of a genius
　That searches with light.

White by the fountain
　Sit the calm seven;
Unto their joyance
　Its music is given.

The world looketh on,
  And still wonders in vain,
As they go out and in,
  And find pasture again.

DOUBLES AND BUBBLES.

"Hey, rub-a-dub!
   Three maids in a tub!
  And who do you think was there?
   The butcher, the baker,
   The candlestick-maker,
  And all of them gone to the fair."

STRONG hands are in the washing-tubs;
  Gay heads, the labor scorning,
Make holiday between the rubs,
  And sport of Monday morning.

Three maids? That 's *your* arithmetic.
  The child that met the poet
Would still to her own counting stick:
  "We 're seven; I surely know it!"

The boatman ferried over three
    Across the haunted river;
And only guessed it by his fee,
    And wondered at the giver.

And Betsey, Jane, and Mary Ann,—
    No more your sense discovers?
Well, rub your insight if you can,
    And reckon up the lovers!

Count Jane with her stout cleaver knight,
    And Betsey with the baker;
And Mary Ann in dreamy light
    Beside the candle-maker.

Yet of the six no soul is there,
    For all your wakened vision!
In the charmed circle of the Fair
    They walk their Fields Elysian!

The work goes on by board and bench, —
    Hard tax of human sinning, —
But hearts thro' labor-chinks still wrench
    Some joy of their beginning.

In the close limit that confines
    Our getting and our giving,
Unless we read between the lines,
    What should we do with living?

FUNERAL HOLIDAY.

" Ding, dong, bell,
   The cat's in the well!
   Who put her in? Little John Green.
   Who pulled her out? Great John Stout!"

THERE was never a drama of sorrow
   But good folks might be found, I'm afraid,
Who a queer satisfaction could borrow
   From the parts of importance they played.

There is war for four years in the nation:
   There are havoc and panic abroad:
Comes a tempest; a wild conflagration:
   Great souls go up home to their God.

How the tall I's spring thick in the spell-
    ing! —
  I knew, or I saw, or I said! —
How the small ones turn out to the swelling
  Each splendor of final parade!

How many are left, we may wonder,
  Heart-mournful for that which befell?
How many would wish back the blunder
  When the Cat has got into the Well!

Nay, more; if with infinite bother
  And peril, poor Puss is got out,
Somehow, one boy seems famous as t' other,
  John Green is as big as John Stout!

See, now! let me tell you a story
  Of something which happened in sooth;
That shows with how fearless a glory
  The children and simple speak truth.

Biddy came to her mistress refulgent;
  A whole sunrise of smiles on her face;
With "M'am, could ye be so indulgent
  Jist to shpare me the day, if ye plase?

" It 's me cousin that 's dead, — Kate
      M'Gawtherin, —
  Was married to Barnaby Roach;
An' I 'd want, — but I hates to be both-
      erin', —
  Three shillin's to pay for the coach!"

And so we were minus our dinners;
  And all that deplorable day
We fasted, like penitent sinners,
  While Biddy the cook was away.

But she came when the sunset was gleam-
      ing;
  And her story she gleefully told;
Disdaining all dolorous seeming,
  In a way that was good to behold.

Each loving and sad recollection
 Of the late Mrs. Barnaby Roach
Quite absorbed in the single reflection
 That she " wint wid himsel' in the coach!"

"For he thrated me, faith, like a lady,
 An' he paid me me fare, an' ahl;
An' he tould me that I, Bridget Brady,
 Was the charm of the funeral!"

DISROBED.

───

" There was a little woman, as I 've heard **tell,**
   She went to market her eggs for to sell:
   She went to market all on a market day,
   And she fell asleep on the king's highway.

" There came a little peddler, his name was **Stout;**
   He cut off her petticoats round about:
   He cut off her petticoats up to her knees,
   And the poor little woman began for to **freeze.**

" She began to shiver, and she began to cry,
   Lawk-a-mercy on me! sure it is n't I!
   But if it be I, as I think it ought to be,
   I 've got a little dog at home, and he knows me !"

1 THINK of a poor, tired Soul,
   That has trodden, up and down,
The tradeways of this busy life,
   To and from its market town,

Till, traffic and toil all past,
    At the silent close of the day,
She lies down, weary and worn, at last,
    On the king's highway; —

The highway that brings all home,
    Never a one left out; —
And in her sleep doth a Stranger come
    Who cuts her garments about.
Cuts the life-tatters away,
    All the old rags and the stain;
And leaves the Soul 'twixt her night and
        day,
    To waken again.

Slowly she wakens, and strange;
    Strange and scared she doth seem;
Marvelling at the mystical change
    Come over her in her dream.

' Where is my life?" she cries,
"That which I knew me by?
Something is here in an unknown guise:
   Can it be I?

" I wonder if anything is:
   Or if I am anything:
Did ever a Soul come bare as this
   From its earthward marketing?
Let me think down into the past;
   Bethink me hard in the cold;
Find me something to stand by fast;
   Something to hold!"

She thinks away back to the morning,
   To something she loved and knew;
And over her doubt comes dawning
   Sense of the dear and true.

" I do n't know if it be I," she sighs;
  " But if after all it be,
There 's a little heart at home in the skies,
  And he 'll know me! "

JACK AND JILL.

> " Jack and Jill
> Went up the hill,
> To draw a pail of water:
> Jack fell down
> And broke his crown,
> And Jill came tumbling after."

JACK and Jill went up the hill,
　　When the world was young, together.
Jack and Jill went up the hill,
　　In Eden ways and weather.
She to seek out blessed springs,
　　He to bear the burden:
Nature their sole choice of things,
　　Love their only guerdon.
That was all the simple creatures knew.

Jack and Jill come down the hill,
  In the world's full years, together.
Jack and Jill come down the hill,
  And there is stormy weather.
'T is all about the *pail*, you see;
  The sweet springs are behind them:
Empty-handed seemeth she
  Who only helped to find them.
Jill would like to swing a bucket, too.

O'er the hillside coming down,
  Eagerly and proudly,
Sparkling trophies to the town
  To bear, she clamors loudly.
But, in face of all the town,
  Challenging its laughter,
Many a Jack comes tumbling down.
  Shall the Jills come after?
Is that what the women want to do?

Listen! When on heights of life
  Hidden pools He planted,
God to Adam and his wife
  Wise division granted.
Gave his son the pitcher broad
  For wealth and weight of water;
But the quick divining-rod
  Confided to his daughter.
Ah, if men and women only knew!

CASUS BELLI.

Impromptu, July, 1870.

" The sow came in with the saddle;
The little pig rocked the cradle;
The dish jumped up on the table
To see the pot swallow the ladle;
The spit that stood behind the door
Threw the pudding-stick on the floor.
'Odsplut!' said the gridiron,
Can't you agree?
I'm the head constable,
Bring 'em to me.'"

Spain came in with an empty throne;
The little prince rocked his German cradle.
"No, no," he said;
And he shook his head;
"I am well content to be let alone."

All the dishes on pantry-ledge
And shelf, and table, were up on edge,
  To see how the Pot,
   Simmering hot,
Would foam at the dip of the threatening
  ladle.

Nothing befell for a minute or so
(Nobody chose to be first, you know),
Till the royal spit, with an angry frown,
Threw a little pudding-stick down.
" Odsplut! " shouts Emperor Gridiron,
  Hissing for a broil,
" Those folks that stand behind the door
  Are getting up a coil!
1 've red Fire panting at my feet;
  I thought how things would be!
I 'm creation's constable,
  Bring the world to me! "

THE DAYS THAT ARE LONG.

"I'll sing you a song
   Of the days that are long;
Of the woodcock and the sparrow;
   Of the little dog
   That burnt his tail,
And he shall be whipt to-morrow."

THAT is the song the world sings
   Of the long bright days:
That is the way she evens things,
   Portions, and pays.

The dog that let his tail burn,
   Proving one pain,
Shall be whipt next day, that he may learn
   Wisdom again.

That is the song the world sings
  To sin and sorrow:
Over her limit her hard lash flings
  Into God's morrow.

Measures His dear divine grace
  In compass narrow:
Counts for nothing the infinite days;
  Forgets the sparrow.

The world sings only a half song;
  Leaves our hearts sore:
Heaven, in the time that is tender and long,
  Will sing us more.

THREESCORE AND TEN.

"How many miles to Babylon?
  Threescore and ten.
 Can I get there by candle-light?
  Yes, and back again."

How many miles of the weary way?
  Threescore miles and ten.
Where shall I be at the end of the day?
  You shall be back again.

You shall prove it all in the lifelong round;
  The joy, and the pain and the sinning;
And at candle-light your soul shall be found
  Back — at its new beginning.

142

Down in his grave the old man lies;
   In from the earthward wild,
At the open door of Paradise
   Enters a little child.

TWO LITTLE BLACKBIRDS

"Two little blackbirds sat upon a stone;
  One flew away, and then there was one ;
  The other flew after and then there was none
  So the poor stone was left all alone."

One of these little birds back again flew ;
  The other came after, and then there were two ;
  Says one to the other, pray, how do you do ?
  Very well, thank you, and, pray, how are you ?

A STONE is the barest fact :
    But living and wonderful things
  Gather to earthly occasion and act
    With folded or parting wings.

Birds of the air are they, —
   Our knowledge, our thought, our love, —
And the ethers in which they win their way
   Are breaths of the heaven above.

Some place and point of the hour, —
   The same little fact for two, —
Who knoweth the lasting wonder and power
   It holdeth for me and you ;

Away in the long-past years,
   With trifle of merest chance,
Keeping, through losing, and blinding, and
      tears,
   The key of its circumstance ?

I, left to the narrowed earth, —
   You into the great heaven gone, —

And things of our sharing, — our work, our
    mirth, —
  So lonely to brood upon!

Yet ever, when thought recurs,
  With hardly a reckoning why,
To some old, small memory, straightway stirs
  That sound of wings in the sky ;

And like birds to a resting-place, —
  No longer one, but the two, —
Alight the remembrances, face to face,
  Alive between me and you ;

And heaven grows real and dear,
  And earth widens up to heaven ;
And all that had vanished, and stayed so
    near,
  In one marvellous glimpse is given.

For memory is return :
   Ourselves are what we have been :
And what we have been together, we learn
   Our life doth continue in.

Spread, then, the angel wings !
   I lose you not as you go ;
Since heart finds heart in the uttermost
      things
   Two thoughts may revisit so !

TAFFY.

―――――――

"Taffy was a Welshman,
　　Taffy was a thief;
Taffy came to my house
　　And stole a piece of beef ·
I went to Taffy's house,
　　Taffy was n't at home;
Taffy came to my house
　　And stole a marrow bone.
I went to Taffy's house,
　　Taffy was in bed;
I took the marrow bone,
　　And beat about his head."

OLD Time came unto my house of clay,
And pilfered its pride of flesh away:

I knocked at the doors of the years in vain
To ask for its goodliness again.

Old Time came unto me yet once more,
For crueller theft than he thieved before;
Stealing the very marrow and bone
That the strength of my life was builded on.

Old Time! At last thou shalt lie in thy bed,
And thy years and days be buried and
　　dead;
And the strength of the life to come shall
　　be
In the great revenge I will have of thee!

MARGERY DAW.

"See, saw! Margery Daw
Sold her bed, and lay upon straw;
Sold her straw, and lay upon dirt;
Was n't she a good-for-naught?"

O MARGERY DAW! Mistress Margery Daw!
Not yours the sole lapse that the world ever
saw!
In precisely such willful gradation
I fear me religion and morals and law
Go down, step by step, to the dirt through
the straw,
In the church and the mart and the na-
tion.

150

A yielding of that, and a dropping of this,—

("With straw fresh and plenty, pray what
    is amiss?

The bed may be wider and cleaner;")

Ah, that's as you make it, and shake it,
    you'll find;

And with slumber forgetful, and luxury
    blind,

What you rest in grows meaner and
    meaner.

'In righteousness walking," the Scripture
    verse goes,—

'They rest in their beds," and find blessed
    repose;

And the beautiful contrary diction

Is neither Isaiah's mistake, nor a word

At random declared, to be scoffingly heard,

But a truth in the freedom of fiction.

O Margery Daw ! Mistress Margery Daw !
It shall always be gospel, what always was
    law :
  Some bed-making none may dispense
    with, —
In dust of the earth, or in heart of the
    heaven, —
And to soul of mankind shall no Sabbath be
    given
  Save that it lies down and contents with.

TROUBLED WITH RATS

"Pretty John Watts,
  We are troubled with rats;
Will you drive them out of the house?
    There are mice, too, in plenty,
    Who feast in the pantry;
    But let them stay,
    And nibble away;
What harm in a little brown mouse?"

A CURIOUS puzzle haunts
  The brain of the commentator,
Whether John Watts, perchance,
  Be preacher or legislator

We 're troubled with rats, we cry :
 And who shall drive out the vermin ?
Let senate and pulpit try :
 Urge edict, and scourge with sermon.

They steal, they riot, they slay :
 They are noisy, they are noisome :
Mice in the pantry, you say ?
 Ah, those little things are toysome !

They only nibble, you see ;
 They only frolic and scamper :
What harm can it possibly be
 A little brown mouse to pamper ?

They 're not of the race, John Watts !
 From them we need no protection ;

They will never develop to rats,
   By survival or selection.

And yet, John Watts! John Watts!
   Whether in closet or highway,
I doubt me that mice and rats
   Are akin, in some sort of sly way;

And as long as the world sins on,
   That the odds will be but a quibble
Between the deeds that are done
   By brutes that devour — or nibble!

LITTLE ROBIN REDBREAST.

Little Robin Redbreast sat upon a tree;
Up went the pussy-cat, down came he:
Down came the pussy-cat, away Robin ran;
Says little Robin Redbreast, catch me if you can!

Little Robin Redbreast hopped upon a spade;
Pussy-cat jumped after him, and then he was afraid;
Little Robin chirped and sung, and what did pussy say
Pussy said, Me-ow! Me-ow! and Robin flew away."

LITTLE Robin Redbreast sat upon a tree,
Heartsome and glad;
The cheer of life, in the green of life, what
ever so blithe may be?
Fol de rol, de rol, lad!

Up went the pussy-cat, and down came
    he, —
    Woe befall for the claws, lad !
The care of life, and the fear of life, it
    creepeth so stealthily, —
      So threatsome and sad !
    And woe befall for the claws, lad !

Down came the pussy-cat, away Robin
    ran,
      In his scarlet clad ;
There may be a day for running away, for
    redcoated bird or man.
      Fol de rol, de rol, lad !
Says little Robin Redbreast, Catch me if
    you can !
    Two merry legs to the four, lad !

A quick, bold pair, that scampers fair, is
    part of the saving plan,
      And a match for the pad
   Aprowl on the pitiless four, lad!

Little Robin Redbreast hopped upon a
    spade;
      This is n't so bad!
All of leafy green, and for joy, I ween, the
    world was never made.
      Fol de rol, de rol, lad!
Pussy-cat jumped after him, and then he
    was afraid;
   Ah, what 's the use of all, lad?
There 's death in our work, there s fear to
    lurk in the places where we played.
      What help 's to be had?
   And what is the use of all, lad?

Little Robin chirped and sung, the same
  brave roundelay;
    There 's room to be glad!
There 's always a light behind the night;
  there 's never a will but a way;
    Fol de rol, de rol, lad!
Little Robin chirped and sung, and what did
  pussy say?
    Creeping, and stretching the claws, lad?
Pussy said, O-w! P-shaw! Me-ow! for
  Robin was off and away.
    There 's wings to be had!
  And fol de rol for the claws, lad!

WHEELBARROW BROKE.

When I was a bachelor, I lived by myself,
And all the bread and cheese I got I put upon a shelf.
The rats and the mice, they made such a strife,
I was forced to go to London to get me a wife.

The streets were so broad, and the lanes were so nar
　　row
I was forced to bring my wife home in a wheelbarrow.
The wheelbarrow broke, and my wife had a fall,
Down came wheelbarrow, wife, and all."

OF course it did.   Whatever could you pos-
　　sibly expect, sir ?
You chose a quite peculiar style to cherish
　　and protect, sir !

160

Your resource in emergency commands my
    admiration,
But I wonder was it want — or excess — of
    calculation,
    That the wheelbarrow broke?

The one-wheeled way gave out, you say?
    Indeed, I should have guessed so,
From the very frank preamble of your pre-
    cious manifesto!
When all the bread and cheese you got you
    shut up in your closet,
Driving such single-blessed team, what
    strange amazement was it
    That your wheelbarrow broke?

You were managing quite finely till the rats
    and mice got at it,

And forced you to the slow resolve, how-
    e'er you might combat it
With other prompting, that a wife must be
    your choice of crosses
In a world of moth and rust and thieves,
    and all provoking losses?
      Yes, — the wheelbarrow broke.

When the scramble and the screed began,
    you fain would share your trouble,
But in no other sense, it seems, arrange for
    going double ;
The generous thoroughfares of life were too
    wide for your barrow,
And the single footpath in the lane you
    plodded was too narrow
      For a couple in a yoke.

The old plan was a careful one; but it could
    never carry
New needs; you should have thought of
    that before you thought to marry;
And still you strove to push it through,
    with many a frown and grumble,
Till the poor little wife and all had got a
    dreadful tumble,
    When the wheelbarrow broke.

Broke midway in the struggle: a providen-
    tial mystery:
The usual meek accounting-for of such mis-
    handled history:
As if it were the method of the wisdom and
    the glory
To run the earth on one wheel, — and each
    small earthly story, —
    Till the wheelbarrow broke!

Ah, friend ! of God's mechanics you mistake
  the grand solution ;
On no weak, single centre runs the perfect
  revolution ;
But one circuit round the sun, — one self-
  circling for the planet, —
And one divine consent of both, — so first
  the power began it,
   And creation was bespoke.

Be sure you must in everything waste hope
  and love and labor,
Moving cheaply by yourself, — nowise
  greatly with your neighbor.
Cease, then, with such ill-balance in the
  ways of life to wraxle,
And put an equal-turning wheel on each
  end of your axle,
   Since your wheelbarrow 's broke !

THE FOOTPATH WAY

"Jog on, jog on, the footpath way,
    And merrily jump the stile, O !
A merry heart goes all the day,
    Your sad one tires in a mile, O!"

Who goes to-day by the footpath way,
When with ocean leagues the steamships
        play,
And under mountains and over plains
Runs the level thunder of the trains?

Who goes to-day by the footpath way,
When the very babies despise great A,

165

And swallow, with supercilious smiles,
Whole sentences, like young crocodiles?

Who goes to-day by the footpath way,
Waiting for good things until he can pay,
When with mortgage and loan and instal-
    ment plan,
Life is let furnished to every man?

Who goes to-day by the footpath way,
When Moses made awful mistakes, they
    say,
And the story of all that began and is
Never happened according to Genesis?

Who goes to-day by the footpath way,
Alone and straitened, with care and de
    lay,

When the world, grown wiser by grace of
    God,
Rolls assured toward heaven on the cause-
    way broad ?

When things are thus since they must be so,
And nobody stands by himself, you know,
And none may jog onward, and none may
    fall
But by force that prevails in the general ?

And what are the odds of tear or smile,
Or whether we merrily leap the stile
Or tumble helpless, since over we must,
And the end of all is the " dust to dust ? "

Well, — take it so ; yet the footpath way
Doth its line through every thoroughfare
    lay ;

The tramp of the legion may seem to efface,
But the single treading hath left its trace.

You may rush by steam with a seven-league
    stride,
Yet the footpath way 's in the railroad
    ride ;
Each goes his own gait, and clears his own
    stiles,
And lives by inches, while driven by miles.

You may scorn your penny, and spend your
    pound,
No less 't will appear, when the day comes
    round,
That farthing by farthing the score was
    made,
And unto the uttermost shall be paid.

And Moses will stand when philosophies
    drop,
And Huxley and Darwin have shut up
    shop;
For whatever you jump, and however you
    jog,
You can't get away from the decalogue.

Then with faith and fear in the footpath
    way,
And with steadfast cheer, trudge on, we
    say ;
For if ever earth into the kingdom rolls,
T will be by the saving of single souls !

UP A TREE.

"Oh dear, what can the matter be?
    Two old women got up in an apple-tree :
        One came down,
    And the other stayed up till Saturday."

I SUPPOSE you wonder how it should be
That two old ladies got up in a tree :
Did you never chance the exploit to see ?

Perhaps you have noticed pussy-cat go,
With a wrathful look, and a way not
        slow,
And a tail very big, and a back up —
    so ⌒ ?

170

DISCORD

a. Hoppin.

Well, that is the type of the thing I mean;
And the apple-bearer, since earth was
    green,
The tree of our trouble hath always been.

So when " human warious " fails to agree,
There stands the old stem of iniquity,
And one or both will be " up a tree."

Each in her style : some are stately and
    stiff ;
Some hiss and spit, and are up in a whiff ;
And some hunch along in a moody miff.

It does n't much matter, however it be ;
The best of people may get up the tree ;
The question is, when they 'll come down,
    you see!

An offenseless one will descend straightway;
One half in the wrong for a while may stay;
Clear curstness will roost till the judgment
    day !

THE CROOKED MAN.

"There was a crooked man,
  And he went a crooked mile ;
  He found a crooked sixpence
  Against a crooked stile :
  He bought a crooked cat,
  Which caught a crooked mouse ;
  And they all lived together
  In a little crooked house."

ONCE begin with a crook,
  You 'll go on with a crook ;
Crooked ways, crooked luck, crooked peo
    ple.

Crooked eyes, crooked mind,
Crooked guideposts will find;
Yes, a crook in the very church-steeple!

The first mile you make
The initial will take
For all the long leagues that shall follow:
Right and left, fork and swerve,
Any turn that will serve,
Up and down, betwixt hummock and hol·
low.

If you pause at a stile
Or a fence for a while,
Some twist must compel or invite you:
Even sin, I 've a doubt,
Were it straight out and out,
Could hardly persuade or delight you.

And a shave, or a bend,
Or a nick, must commend,
For you, every quarter and nickel :
Right pure from the mint,
There were no magic in 't
Your trick-loving finger to tickle.

Crooked money will buy
But a crook or a lie,
Whatever the ware that you deal in ;
Your position in life,
Your companions, your wife,
Or even a playfellow feline.

And as thief catches thief
In the common belief,
Be the creature a cat or a woman,
The crooked shall still

Find the crooked at will,
And you'll see the old saw sayeth true, **man.**

In kin, neighbors, house,
In a servant or mouse,
She will always put paw on her likeness :
The same rule runs through,
For the false and the true, —
Straight to straight, and oblique to oblique-
ness.

So together, you see,
As you build, you shall be,
Every line of the mould in the casting ;
And a nice little world
You'll have made, when you've
curled
And squirmed to your state everlasting !

THE FOUR WINDS.

"When the wind is in the east,
'T is neither good for man nor beast;
When the wind is in the north,
The skillful fisher goes not forth;
When the wind is in the south,
It blows the bait in the fishes' mouth;
When the wind is in the west,
Then 't is at the very best."

LIFE, like the earth, to the east doth run,
Turning her face to the face of the sun.
The wind that is contrary, as she goes,
Is always the bitterest wind that blows;
Smiting the kiss of the shining away,
And beating backward the beautiful day.

177

The wind that comes from the icy pole
Shutteth up hope in the human soul;
Chiding the heart, and forbidding the will,
And blasting our very beginnings with ill.
Oh, the wind of the north, on its terrible
    path,
Is the wind of wreck, and despair, and
    wrath !

The breath that blows from the climes of
    ease,
From the isles of spice and the bread-fruit
    trees,
With its unearned flavors to fill the mouth;
The zephyr that sends from the idle south
Its soft beguiling and treacherous touch, —
Let the soul in her struggle be shy of
    such !

But the wind that springs from the hind-
 ward side,
And as earth rolls under sweeps over the
 tide ;
The gust that is vigorous, brave, and true,
Backing you up in whatever you do,
Keen and impelling, the wind of the west, —
Ah, well saith the legend, that breeze is the
 best.

THE PIPER AND THE COW.

"There was a piper had a cow,
    And he had naught to give her :
So he took up his pipes, and he played her a tune,
    Consider, cow, — consider !

The cow considered very well,
    And gave the piper a penny ;
And bade him play the other tune, —
    Corn-rigs are bonny."

GOOD folks of the pen, I am sure you 'll
        agree
That author and publisher here we may see :
The Piper plays tunes 'twixt the world and
        the Cow,

And he has, at the same time, the care of
    the mow :
When the crop in the barn shows but little
    to feed her,
To the Cow quoth the Piper, Consider, con·
    sider !

The Cow is a creature that cheweth the cud ;
Recalleth the hill-sides, with daisies be-
    stud,
The sweet running waters, the breezes at
    play,
While mournfully munching the last lock of
    hay :
All the world that she knoweth of fra-
    grance and stir
Sealeth up in those dry stems its juices for
    her.

So it cometh, forsooth, that because she can
    chew
People think it is all she can hunger to do :
Neither Public nor Piper doth fully allow
For the interdependence of mood and of
    mow,
Or see how perplexing it may be, alas,
For a Cow to consider between hay and
    grass !

Howbeit, if Mooly considereth well,
And giveth the Piper good milk for to sell,
The Piper he maketh his own modest
    penny, —
Just one at a time, till he hath a great
    many ;
And during the while this is coming to pass
Fresh fodder grows plenty, and delicate
    grass.

Once more life's a pasture; the season is
    June;
The pipes play up cheerly the bonny-rig
    tune;
The Cow is in clover; the buttercups hold
Right up to her chin their probation of
    gold;
But she knows, all the same, how 't will be
    when they bid her
The next year, as last year, Consider, con-
    sider!

BEHIND THE LOG.

"Pussy sits behind the log; how can she be fair?
Then comes in the little dog: Pussy, are you there?
So, so, dear mistress pussy, pray tell me how you do!
I thank you, little dog, I am very well just now."

BEHIND the log, in the reek and mould,
    How many poor things are there,
Who else might be sought, and caressed
      and told,
    So tenderly, they were fair!

Behind the log, ah, behind the log,
    Such only can tell us how
They are glad of a word from a little dog
    Who pauses to say Bow-wow!

SHOE AND FIDDLE.

"Cock-a-doodle-doo!
 My dame has lost her shoe;
 My master's lost his fiddlestick,
 And does n't know what to do."

WHO's crowing, I wonder, to spread such
 a scandal
Of the blithe-tripping dame who hath
 dropped off her sandal,
And seemeth all sad and forlornly to
 shirk,
Where she used, in good humor, to dance
 at her work?

185

Perhaps honest chanticleer simply may
  glory
In faithfully giving both sides of the story ·
And scorning the loss of the lady to tell
Without owning the miss of the master as
  well.

For how, when the fiddlestick 's gone, can
  be played
The music, without which the dancing is
  stayed ?
When the man 's out of tune, the dear
  woman, 't is plain,
Must wait till he graciously strikes up again.

Let him hunt for his bow, then, and rosin it
  too,
(If really he 'd like to be told what to do ;)

And I think, with the fiddling, 't will surely
be found

All else will come right for the merry-go-
round

SWING, SWONG

_____

" Swing, Swong!
　The days are long!
　Up hill, and down dale ;
　Butter is made in every vale."

Your day will come, though it arrive but
　　slowly ;
There 's cream in all life, set however
　　lowly ;
And if, as Goose philosophy, you doubt
　　it,
Hear what the little hen found out about
　　it : —

" Kroo ! kroo !   I 've cramp in my legs,
   Sitting so long atop of my eggs ;
   Never a minute for rest to snatch ;
   I wonder when they are going to hatch !

" Cluck ! cluck ! listen ! tseep !
   Down in the nest there 's a stir and a
     peep.
   Everything comes to its luck some day ;
   I 've got chickens ! What will folks say ? "

SHUTTLECOCK.

" Here we go up, up, up,
  And here we go down, down, downy ;
  Here we go backward and forward,
  And here we go round, round, roundy."

BATTLEDORE and shuttlecock !
    Hither, and thither, and yon :
Never a flight without a knock,
    And so the world goes on.

Shuttlecock and battledore !
    When will it all be done,—
The life of the buffet and beat be o'er,
    And the life of the wings begun ?

THE MAN IN THE WILDERNESS.

"The man in the wilderness, he asked me
  How many strawberries grew in the sea:
  I answered him, as I thought good,
  As many red herrings as grew in the wood."

Of the face of the world they have found
      it out
    By what they must fetch and do;
Of the heart of the world they dispute and
    doubt,
    And yet it is just as true.

Your fish is wholesome, and live, and clean,
    And my little fruit is fair;

Though the earth's good Maker might never
    mean
    That both should be everywhere.

And all for the want of a thought like this,
    It comes, and it can but be,
That many a soul 's in the wilderness,
    And many adrift at sea.

PRAE AND POST.

"The man in the moon
Came down too soon
To inquire the way to Norwich;
The man in the south,
He burnt his mouth
With eating cold plum porridge."

THE moony men are always in a hurry
That puts sedater people in a flurry;
They get their theories through other media
Than facts of gazetteer or cyclopædia;
And then, by some unknown, preposterous
    gateway,
Rush forth to claim the realizing straight-
    way.

193

Just think of lighting on a foreign planet,
Asking for Norwich before folks began it!

But then, those sleepy souls at the equator
Lose just as much, you see, by starting
  later;
Never strike in while anything is hot, —
Wait till the porridge is all out o' the
  pot; —
And through their indolence and easy fool-
  ing
Burn their mouths, figuratively, in the cool-
  ing!

Too soon, too slow, there 's nothing comes
  out even;
The very sun that travels through the
  heaven

Heels o'er the line, now this way and now
        that,
And only twice a year can hit it pat.
Even your two eyes make a parallax,
And might mislead you on two different
        tracks ;
Between them both, the moral, I suppose,
Is that each man should follow his **own**
        nose !

QUITE CONTRARY.

"Mistress Mary, quite contrary,
 How does your garden grow?
With silver bells, and cockle shells,
 And tulips, all of a row."

PRITHEE, tell me, Mistress Mary,
Whence this rhyme of "quite contrary"?
Why should Mother Goose, beholding
All these pleasant blooms unfolding, —
Every prim and pretty border
Standing in such shining order, —
Looking o'er the lovely rows,
Ask you "how your garden grows"?

Mary, so precise and chary,
Are you, anyhow, contrary?
While these sweetly perfect lines
Nod their gentle countersigns,
Spending all your strength on this,
Lest the least thing grow amiss,
Weareth some unseen parterre
Quite a different kind of air?

Through your hating of a **weed**
Runs there any ill to seed, —
Thistle-blow of petulance,
Bitter blade of blame, perchance,
Or a flaunting stem of pride,
In that other garden-side ?
Mary, in our women-hearts
Spring such curious counterparts !

Each her home-plot watching wary,
Lest the faultless order vary
By the dropping of a leaf,
Or a blossom come to grief
From the blasting of the storm,
Or the eating of a worm,
Let us both be certain, Mary,
Nothing dearer goes contrary !

ALONG, LONG, LONG.

"As I was going along, long, long,
  A singing a comical song, song, song,
  The lane that I went was so long, long, **long**,
  And the song that I sung was so long, long, **long**,
      And so I went singing along."

It 's all along, and along!
For the earth is bonny, and glad, and wide,
And we 're free to wander, and free to bide,
      And we travel with a song.

It 's long, it 's wearily long!
For the path is narrowed to only a lane;
And we 've sung it over and over again,
      That old, monotonous song.

199

Nay, let us be thankful and strong,

That the breath of life is as long as the day,

And the song is as long as the weariful way,

And so, we 'll go singing along !

FINIS.

" The white dove sat on the castle wall,

I bent my bow, and shoot her I shall,"—

   (The fair bird, truth, and her meanings ;)

" I put her in my glove, both feathers and

      all ; "

(The pretty plumes that her flight let fall ;

   For I bound in a book my gleanings :)

" I laid my bridle upon the shelf, —

If you want any more, you may sing it

      yourself ! '

   (It 's all in the wits and the weenings !)

20

CONCLUSION.

(*EDITORIAL.*)

DOUBTLESS I might go on to quote,

With added paraphrase and note,

Precept on precept, line on line,

To instance here the fact divine

That of her children, far and wide,

Wisdom is always justified.

Yet why oppress with proof of that,

Since " verbum sapienti sat " ?

Suffice it to have struck the vein,

   And shown some specimens of ore ;

If any seek for further gain,

   The mine still holds abundance more.

A mental pickaxe and a biggin

Are all you need to go to diggin'.

For, as the Swedish seer contends,
All things comprise an inner sense;
There's nothing we can write or say,
In howsoever simple way,
But seems a body, built to hide
The soul that straightway is supplied;
And many a fool, and prophet too,
Hath spoken wiser than he knew.

One parting word, and I am gone:
   If I 've prevailed to make you see
   These things as they appear to me,
Then have I proved my Goose a Swan;
And I, small fledgling of the line,
   Yet proud to bear the ancient name,
May, for this ancestress of mine,
   Claim place upon the page of fame; —
That not a bard of Saxon tongue
More true to nature ever sung:

More surely soothed, more deeply taught,
Or passing fact more keenly caught;
And that — exalted side by side
With him of Avon, in the pride
And love of millions — we should lay
The tribute at her feet to-day
That owns her, in this latter age,
Goose, truly, — but, in savor, Sage!

www.ingramcontent.com/pod-product-compliance
Lightning Source LLC
Chambersburg PA
CBHW030115030726
47498CB00007B/2400